W9-COY-799

Rosie and the Rustlers

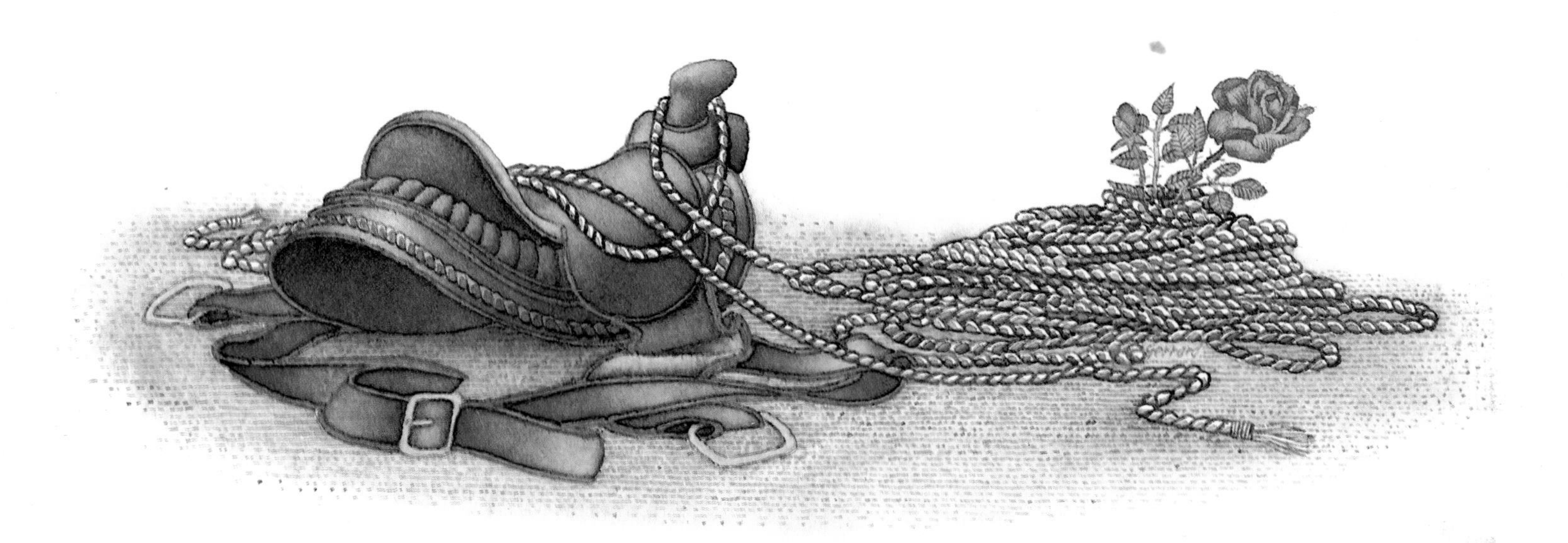

ROY GERRARD

FARRAR STRAUS GIROUX NEW YORK

Where the mountains meet the prairie, where the men are wild and hairy,
There's a little ranch where Rosie Jones is boss.
It's a place that's neat and cozy, and the boys employed by Rosie
Work extremely hard, to stop her getting cross.

Next to Rose is Fancy Dan, on his left is Salad Sam,
One-Leg Smith and Singing Sid and Mad McGhee.
And then there's Utah Jim, who looks nice but rather dim —
Quite a decent bunch of boys they seem to me.

In the saddle every day, well, they sure do earn their pay
Doing wrangling and lassoing and such stuff.
When it's windy or it's raining, you won't hear the boys complaining,
For the life they lead makes cowboys pretty tough.

When their hard day's work is done and it's time to have some fun
They all gather in the bunkhouse for the night.
Sam whips up some lovely salads, Sidney sings them charming ballads,
And they serenade till turning out the light.

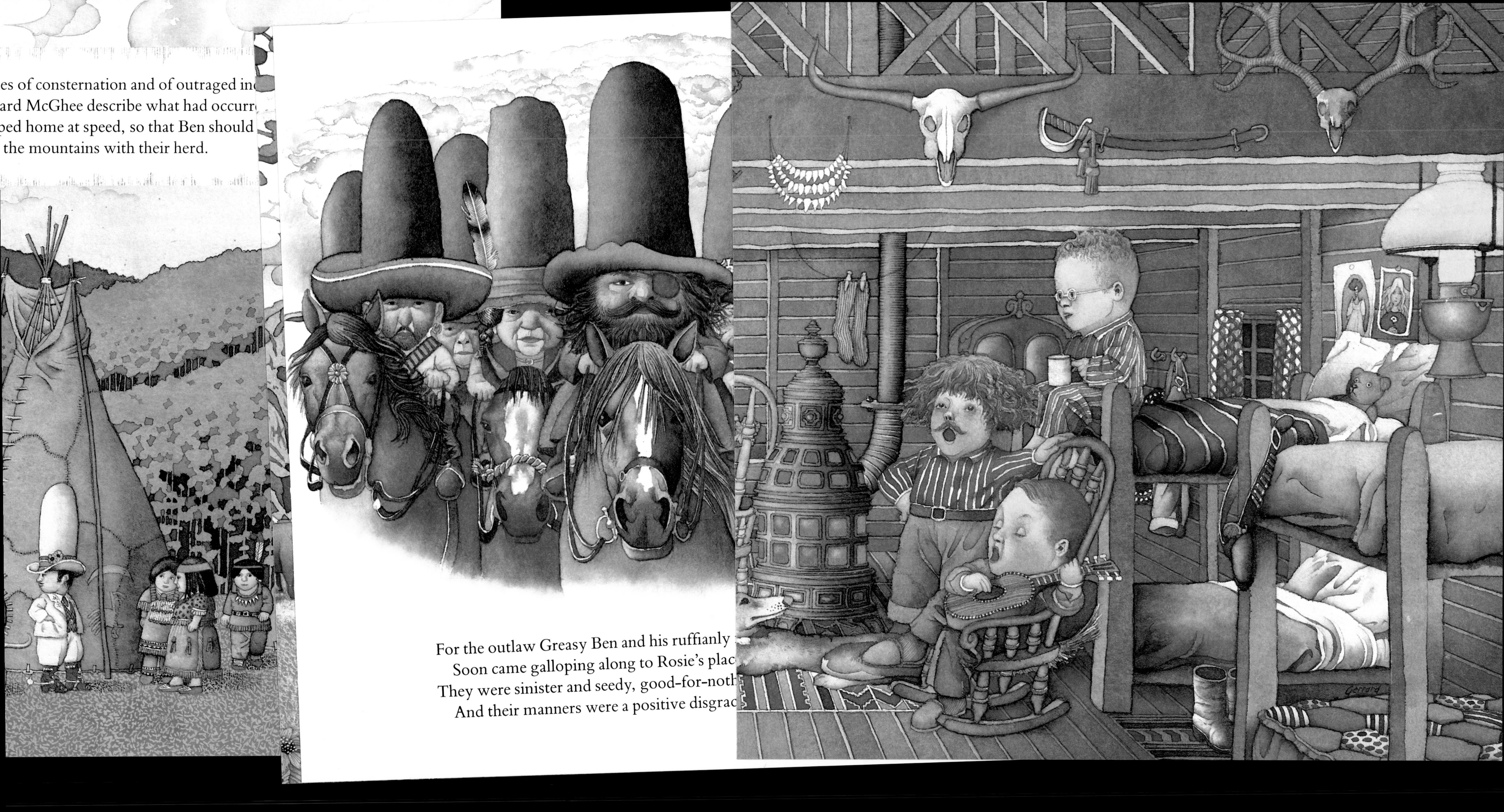

es of consternation and of outraged in
ard McGhee describe what had occurr
ped home at speed, so that Ben should
the mountains with their herd.

For the outlaw Greasy Ben and his ruffianly
Soon came galloping along to Rosie's plac
They were sinister and seedy, good-for-noth
And their manners were a positive disgrac

On the day they went to see their de
They left Mad McGhee behind to
Though they went without a care, t
Which involved McGhee in some

Having spent a restful night, they all woke up feel
Though the ground was hard and lumpy, to be
They put on their hats and jeans, had some coffee
Then they mounted up and hit the trail once mo

Gerrard

With great doggedness and care they searched out the bandits' lair,
Till they found the shack of Ben and all his crew,
And then Rosie and her boys, being sure to make no noise,
Found a hiding place, then wondered what to do.

Rosie Jones was quite enraptured, now the wicked gang was captured
(Though she felt relieved that none had chanced to drown).
So once more they hit the trail, to put Ben and Co. in jail,
And the folks all cheered when Rosie came to town.

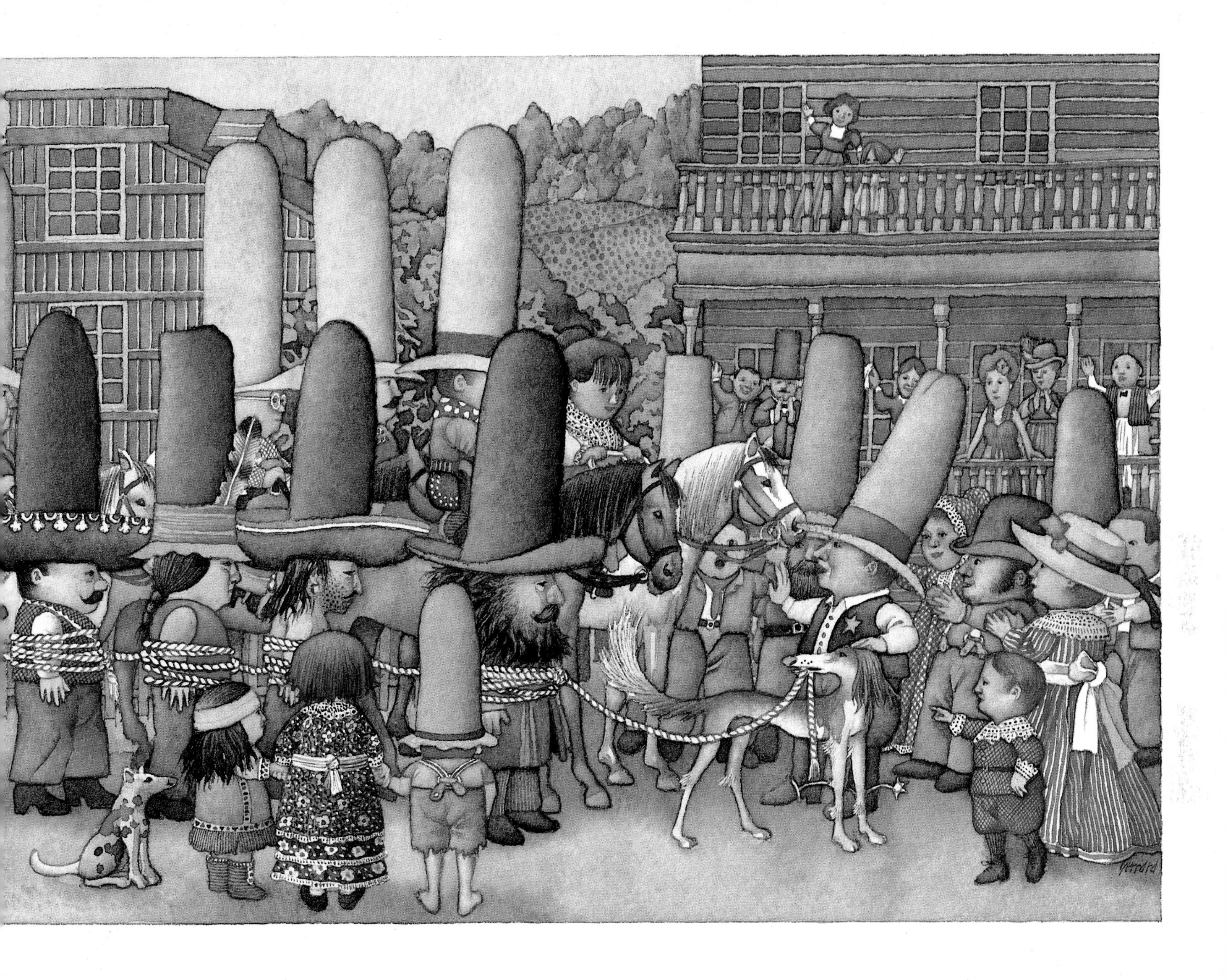

Then the sheriff was well pleased that the bandits had been seized,
And the townsfolk gathered round them to applaud.
Rosie's gallant little band became famed throughout the land,
And they got five hundred dollars as reward.

Rosie held a celebration for the local population
To express her thanks for what her friends had done.
There was dancing in the street, and delicious things to eat,
So that everybody had enormous fun.

Where the mountains meet the prairie, where the men are wild and hairy,
There's a little ranch where Rosie reigns supreme.
Where the grass could not be greener, where the air could not be cleaner,
Life is happy, life is peaceful — it's a dream.

First published in Great Britain by Victor Gollancz Ltd, 1989
Library of Congress catalog card number: 89–45499
Printed in Hong Kong
First American edition, 1989
Second printing, 1989